TEN REDNECK BABIES

TEN REDNECK BABIES

A Southern Counting Book

David Davis

Illustrated by Sue Marshall Ward

PELICAN PUBLISHING COMPANY

Gretna 2004

For Jan Peck, Cerelle Woods, Melissa Russell, Kathryn Lay, Diane Roberts, BJ Stone, Janet Fick, Chris Ford, Tom McDermott, Sue Ward, Deborah Lightfoot, Trish Holland, Amanda Jenkins, and Debra Deur. Also for my editors, Nina Kooij and Cynthia Williams, and for all children everywhere.—D. D.

For Jody Taylor and David Davis, for their confidence. For my writing group and friends, listed above, for their undying support. For my grandchildren, Alex, Katie, Laura, Ashley, Meesha, and Sean—they are inspiring and mischievous. And for my husband and family—they're the best.—S. M. W.

Copyright © 2004
By David Davis

Illustrations copyright © 2004
By Sue Marshall Ward
All rights reserved

The word "Pelican" and the depiction of a pelican are trademarks of Pelican Publishing Company, Inc., and are registered in the U.S. Patent and Trademark Office.

Library of Congress Cataloging-in-Publication Data

Davis, David (David R.), 1948-
    Ten redneck babies / by David Davis ; illustrated by Sue Marshall Ward.
       p. cm.
    Summary: When ten redneck babies stroll to town in this counting book, they find all types of mischief in the golden South.
    ISBN 1-58980-232-2 (hardcover : alk. paper)
    [1. Babies—Fiction. 2. Southern States—Fiction. 3. Counting.] I. Ward, Sue Marshall, 1941- ill. II. Title.

    PZ8.3.D28942Ten 2004
    [E]—dc22

                                                                2003027740

Printed in Singapore

Published by Pelican Publishing Company, Inc.
1000 Burmaster Street, Gretna, Louisiana 70053

TEN REDNECK BABIES

10 redneck babies strolled to town.
One bought a Moon Pie and he sat down.

9 redneck babies running free—
One shinnied up a magnolia tree.

8 redneck babies riding bluetick hounds—
One hid in kudzu on the red dirt ground.

7 redneck babies bounced on hay.
One took a nap on this summer's day.

6 redneck babies cotton pickin'—
One ate a lunch of crisp fried chicken.

5 redneck babies chomped watermelon.
One made tracks—where to? No tellin'!

4 redneck babies buttering grits—
One dropped her plate and pitched a fit.

3 redneck babies fishing a creek—
One caught a catfish and bragged all week.

2 redneck babies chased a squawking hen.
One treed a possum and watched him grin.

1 redneck baby bawled all alone,
So his mama fed him some hot corn pone.

Let's count back up, 'cause we counted down.
Y'all read along for another round!

1 redneck baby fed a mooing calf.
The critter licked him and he began to laugh.

2 redneck babies picked old banjos.
One began to square-dance and tap her toes.

3 redneck babies caught a fat, greased pig.
One picked his teeth with a sweet-gum twig.

4 redneck babies kissed their red-haired maw.
One wound a pocket watch for old grandpaw.

5 redneck babies shelled black-eyed peas.
One sewed patches on his blue-jean knees.

6 redneck babies shed their socks and shoes.
One grabbed a guitar and strummed the blues.

7 redneck babies hoed a garden patch.
One got chiggers and commenced to scratch.

8 redneck babies shared a peanut patty.
One hugged the neck of her redneck daddy.

9 redneck babies in a tin washtub—
One baby's mama gave his ears a scrub.

The tale is over; that much is true.
So I should end it—and I'm fixin' to!

10 redneck babies love the golden South.
This yarn is done, so I'll shut my mouth!